Snow Joke

Also by Bruce Degen

I Said, "Bed!"

Snow Joke

by **BRUCE DEGEN**

Holiday House / New York

Printed and Bound in April 2015 at Tien Wah Press, Johor Bahru, Johor, Malaysia.
The artwork was created with pen and ink, watercolor, colored pencil
and gouache on 140 lb. Arches hot press paper.
www.holidayhouse.com
3 5 7 9 10 8 6 4 2

Library of Congress Cataloging-in-Publication Data
Degen, Bruce, author, illustrator.
Snow joke / by Bruce Degen. — First edition.
pages cm. — (I like to read)
Summary: "After playing mean jokes on Bunny while they romp in the snow,
Red learns how to joke nicely"— Provided by publisher.
ISBN 978-0-8234-3065-9 (hardcover)
[1. Behavior—Fiction. 2. Jokes—Fiction. 3. Squirrels—Fiction.
4. Rabbits—Fiction.] I. Title.
PZ7.D3635Sno 2014
[E]—dc23
2013037253

ISBN: 978-0-8234-3455-8 (paperback)

Snow!

"Hey! Who threw that?"

"That's not funny," said Bunny.

"It's just a joke," said Red.
"Let's make a snowman."

"That's not funny," said Bunny.

"It's just a joke," said Red.

"Let's make snow angels."

“That’s not funny,” said Bunny.

"It's just a joke," said Red.
"Let's go sledding."

"That's not funny!"

"It's just a joke," said Red.
"Let's skate."

Red sped.
Red pushed.

Everyone went to Bunny's house.

But where was Red?

Red was on the step.

"Have some cocoa," said Bunny.

Then Red told a
really good joke.
And everyone liked it.

Red's Joke

What is the best snow joke?

Good friends—

because that's snow joke!

(That's NO JOKE!)

Some More I Like to Read® Books in Paperback

Car Goes Far by Michael Garland

Come Back, Ben by Ann Hassett and John Hassett

Crow Made a Friend by Margaret Peot

Ed and Kip by Kay Chorao

Fireman Fred by Lynn Rowe Reed

Fix This Mess! by Tedd Arnold

Hiding Dinosaurs by Dan Moynihan

I Said, "Bed!" by Bruce Degen

I Will Try by Marilyn Janovitz

Late Nate in a Race by Emily Arnold McCully

Look! by Ted Lewin

Pie for Chuck by Pat Schories

Ping Wants to Play by Adam Gudeon

See Me Dig by Paul Meisel

Sick Day by David McPhail

Snow Joke by Bruce Degen

Visit http://www.holidayhouse.com/I-Like-to-Read/ for more about I Like to Read® books, including flash cards, reproducibles and the complete list of titles.